ZONDERkidz™

Stink Bug Saves the Day!
Copyright © 2008 by Bill Myers
Illustrations © 2008 by Andy J. Smith

Requests for information should be addressed to:
Grand Rapids, Michigan 49530

Library of Congress Cataloging-in-Publication Data
Myers, Bill, 1953-
Stink bug saves the day! : the parable of the Good Samaritan / by Bill Myers ;
illustrated by Andy J. Smith.   p. cm. -- (Bug parables series)
Summary: In this retelling of the Good Samaritan parable, Papa Roly-Poly, left bruised and
wounded after being accosted by a gang of flies, finds help from an unexpected source.
ISBN-13: 978-0-310-71219-0 (printed hardcover)
ISBN-10: 0-310-71219-X (printed hardcover) [1. Insects--Fiction. 2. Good Samaritan (Parable)--
Ficion. 3. Christian life--Fiction. 4. Stories in rhyme.] I. Smith, Andy J., 1975- ill. II. Title.
PZ8.3.M99534Sti 2008   [E]--dc22
2006023519

All Scripture quotations unless otherwise noted are taken from the Holy Bible: New International
Version®. NIV®. Copyright © 1973, 1978, 1984 by International Bible Society. Used by permission of
Zondervan. All rights reserved.

Published in association with the literary agency of Alive Communications, Inc.,
7680 Goddard Street, Suite 200, Colorado Springs, CO 80920

Zonderkidz is a trademark of Zondervan.

Editor: Betsy Flikkema
Art direction & Design: Sarah Molegraaf

Printed in China

08 09 10 11 • 6 5 4 3 2 1

THE BUG PARABLES

Stink Bug Saves the Day!

The Parable of
the Good Samaritan

written by
BILL MYERS

illustrated by
ANDY J. SMITH

ZONDERkidz

ZONDERVAN.com/
AUTHORTRACKER
follow your favorite authors

The Roly-Polys are chillin'
on a family vacation,
headin' out on their wheels,
checkin' out their bug nation.

Just then the motor home
runs out of power.
Its red rubber band
wasn't wound for an hour.

They strip Pop and rob him.

Too bad that's not all.

Because when they finish, they play soccer ball.

He combs his antennae
so he'll look good for God,

and then hears the approach
of a loud marching squad.

Feeling hopeless now,
Pop rolls onto his back.
He just can't believe
they've cut him no slack.

Then all of a sudden
he looks to the sky.
He hears notes of hope
that bring tears to his eyes.

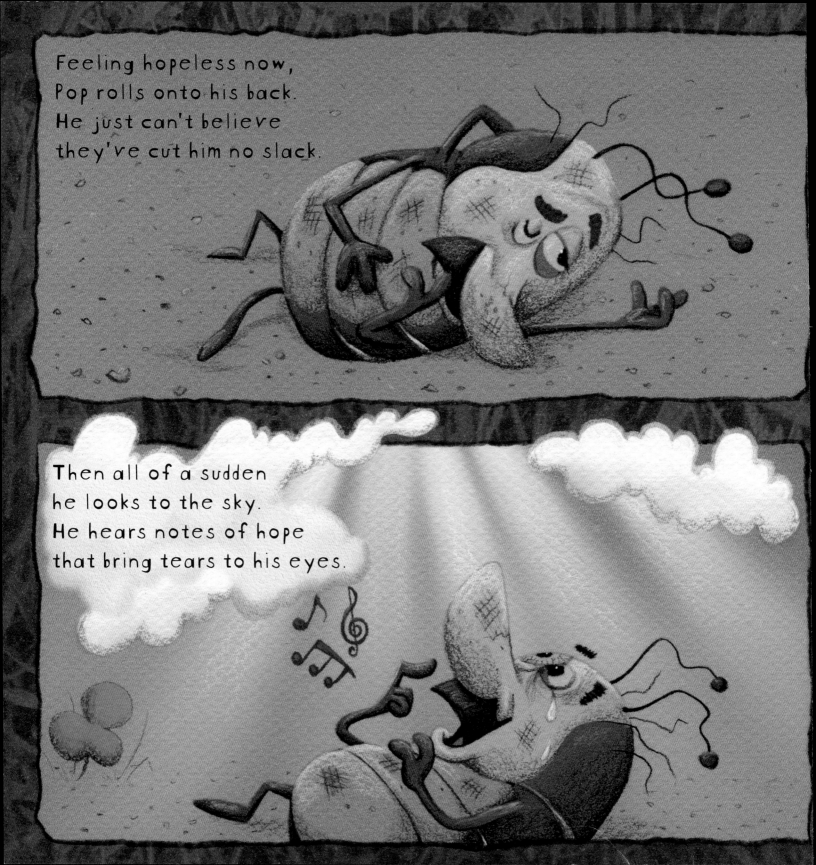

Amazing grace, how sweet the sound,
that makes us awesome people.
We're so much better than the rest
'cause we go to a fancy steeple.

And so off they flutter
up and away.
But not before wishing him—

♪ Have a nice day!

Poor Pop just gives up
and takes his last breath.
Just then he gets wind of
a smell worse than death.

The bug stays to help, giving him comfort that night.

MATCHES

He leaves in the morning.

Please treat this guy right.

Days later Pop's found.
Thank the Lord you're alive!
MATCHES
But how did you get here?
We thought you had died.
Then through his pain, with his jaw wired shut, Pop mumbles his story:
Mumffle mwa meeb wat.